Dead Man Talking

Roddy Doyle

JONATHAN CAPE
LONDON

Published by Jonathan Cape 2015

2 4 6 8 10 9 7 5 3 1

First published in Great Britain in 2015 by
Jonathan Cape
20 Vauxhall Bridge Road,
London SW1V 2SA

www.vintage-books.co.uk

global.penguinrandomhouse.com

A CIP catalogue record for this book is available from the British Library

ISBN 9780224102216

The Random House Group Limited supports The Forest Stewardship Council® (FSC®), the leading international forest-certification organisation. Our books carrying the FSC label are printed on FSC®-certified paper. FSC is the only forest-certification scheme supported by the leading environmental organisations, including Greenpeace. Our paper procurement policy can be found at www.randomhouse.co.uk/environment

FSC www.fsc.org MIX Paper from responsible sources FSC® C016897

Typeset by SX Composing DTP, Rayleigh, Essex
Printed and bound in Great Britain by
CPI Group (UK) Ltd, Croydon, CR0 4YY

Chapter One

I met Joe again the night before his funeral.

Let me explain.

When I was younger than I am now, I knew a man called Joe Murphy. In fact, I knew him before he was a man. I knew him since we were kids.

We were best friends.

But I hadn't seen Joe in nine or ten years. We'd had a fight.

A big fight.

I know what you are thinking. At least, I think I know what you are thinking. 'It must have been about a woman.' But you are wrong. The fight had not been about a woman. It had been about a horse. It had been about a horse and three women.

But the story isn't really about the fight.

I don't know where to start.

I can start in Joe's house, the night before his funeral. Or I can go back to the time when we had the fight. Or I can go all the way back to the time when we were two small boys playing football.

We were best friends, kicking the ball against the side wall of Joe's house. We were both going to play for Manchester United and we were never, ever going to fight.

If I was reading this story, I would want to read about meeting Joe the day before his funeral. Because it is a bit mad. It is not something that happens every day, is it? If it was the day before his funeral, Joe must have been dead.

That is what you are thinking.

And you are right. He was dead.

He was dead. But then he started talking to me.

I don't know where to start.

I don't even know if I want to start.

But I have to.

Chapter Two

Everything was normal.

I drove home from work. I'm a printer.

I *was* a printer.

I drove home and parked the car. I went into the house and kissed my wife, Sarah. It was what I did every day.

'How was work?' she asked.

'Grand,' I said. 'And you?'

'Grand too,' she said.

Sarah worked down the road, in the local supermarket.

We had the dinner – fish and chips. Sarah had got the fish and chips on her way home from work. She had texted me. *Chipper? X.* I had texted her back. *For sure – lol. X.*

'Lovely bit of fish,' I said.

'Yes,' she said. 'And the chips are perfect.'

'Lovely.'

It was not the most exciting chat we ever had. But I need you to know that it was normal.

At least, I thought it was normal.

'I think I'll go for a pint,' I said.

'Grand,' she answered.

This was how it was every night. I went for a pint, just one. And Sarah watched crap on the TV. Then I came home and we would both watch crap together.

I stood up.

'See you later,' I said.

'Yes,' she said. 'Enjoy your pint.'

I got my coat and went to the front door. I put my hand on the handle.

I heard Sarah.

'Pat!'

Her voice was high. She sounded scared, like she had just seen a mouse or something.

'What?' I shouted.

'Pat!'

Now I was scared. I went back to the kitchen.

'What's wrong?'

She was standing now. She was holding her mobile phone.

'It's Joe,' she said.

'Joe who?' I asked.

She shouted at me.

'Joe!'

She looked pale. Her hands were shaking.

I understood now.

'My Joe?' I said.

She nodded.

'Yes.'

Joe had been the best man at our wedding.

'Oh, God,' I said. 'What happened?'

'He's – '

'Dead?'

'Yes,' she said. 'Pat, I'm so sorry.'

She started to cry. And so did I.

She hugged me.

'I'm so sorry,' she said again.

I was glad she didn't say more. She just held me.

'How did you find out?' I asked her.

She held up her phone. I had not heard it ringing when I was going out of the house. But I didn't say anything. I forgot about it. It was not important.

'You are cold,' she said.

But I was not cold. She was. I was shivering – because I was holding a very cold woman.

I let go of Sarah. I stepped back and looked at her, carefully.

'Are you okay?' I asked.

She seemed stiff – solid. Like a statue. A statue made of ice. Green ice.

Then she moved. It was like she moved just an inch. I think it was the light coming through the window. The sun was low outside. It was nearly night, and the sun had gone into my eyes. It had made me think that Sarah looked like ice. But now she was back to normal.

But I know now. Nothing was normal.

Chapter Three

I went for a walk.

Sarah didn't want me to. She looked worried, even a bit angry.

'I need to get some air,' I said.

I needed to move. I did not want to stay still. Walking helped me when I needed to think.

'I'm going,' I said. 'Okay?'

'To the pub?' she asked.

'No.'

She looked happier when I said that.

'Don't worry,' I said. 'I won't go drinking.'

She smiled.

'I wasn't worried,' she said.

I was not a big drinker. But I used to be. It worried Sarah, sometimes. She was afraid I would become a big drinker again.

'I won't be long,' I said. 'Just around the block.'

'Bring the dog,' she said.

It was our joke. We did not have a dog.

I went to the kitchen door. I stopped.

'What happened?' I asked.

'To Joe?'

'Yes.'

'I don't know,' she said. 'Just that he died.'

'Who phoned you?' I asked.

She looked down at the phone.

'It was a text,' she said.

'From who?'

'Oh,' she said. 'Karen.'

Karen was Joe's wife. I had not seen Karen in years.

'She had your phone number?' I asked.

'Someone must have given it to her,' said Sarah.

'Okay.'

I went to the front door. I put my hand on the handle.

It was strange. The last time I was at the front door, I had a friend called Joe who I had not seen in years. I was not thinking about him. Now, just a few minutes later, Joe was dead, and I could think of nothing else.

'Bye,' I shouted.

Sarah didn't answer.

I walked out of the house.

Chapter Four

It was cold that night. It was dark now too. The sun had gone down, behind the houses. I shivered as I walked. I felt sad and guilty – and a bit angry. But, really, I didn't feel anything. I was numb, I think. I felt like I was jet-lagged.

Memories jumped around in my head. It wasn't a line of pictures and sounds, or like a picture album. My memories of Joe were all mashed together.

One big Joe. The child, the adult and the dead man, all in one.

I'd be thinking of the two of us playing football and Joe's adult voice would say, 'That never happened.'

It was raining now. I didn't care. The cold rain cleared my head, a bit. I am bald, so the drops of rain smacked right onto my skull.

I was cold and wet but one warm memory began to grow.

I was in a dusty place. It was dark, but there were thin lines of light. The dust danced in the light. It was brilliant – and hot. Now I could feel

Joe. He was right beside me. I knew where we were now.

'Attics are so cool,' said Joe.

He whispered, because we were not supposed to be there. We were in the attic of my house. My mother had told me never to go up there.

Our eyes were getting used to the dark.

Mam had gone to the shops. My dad was at work and my big sisters were out, doing the stupid stuff that big sisters did. Me and Joe were the only ones in the house. But Mam would be back in a few minutes.

We had climbed up on the ladder. We had carried the ladder – a big steel one – from the back garden.

'There's no floor,' said Joe.

'What?'

We both looked down. Joe was right. There was no real floor. Just thin planks of wood.

Joe put his foot on one plank.

'Careful,' I said.

He put his other foot on the plank beside it. He moved.

'It's easy,' he said. 'Come on.'

I watched him do a funny walk along the planks. He went through the light and dust.

'Brilliant.'

I followed him. He was right. It was easy.

'What are we looking for?' Joe asked.

He didn't whisper now. He nearly shouted. His voice crashed through the dust.

'I don't know,' I said.

'A dead body?'

'Don't think so.'

'Money?'

'Hope so.'

There were boxes up there, and old clothes scattered around.

Something moved.

'What was that?'

'A mouse!'

'A rat!'

'A ghost!'

My foot came off the plank. It landed on something, and went right through. I was falling.

'Joe!'

He grabbed my jumper and pulled me up.

We looked down. My foot had gone through my mam and dad's bedroom ceiling. We looked down through the hole.

'I've made a hole in the ceiling,' I said.

'That's a good big bed,' said Joe. 'Will we jump down?'

Then we heard the door open downstairs. My mam had come home.

I heard her voice.

'Pat? Where are you?'

And Joe jumped.

I was walking towards Joe's house. I saw that now. I wanted to talk to him. I wanted to talk to him about the two of us in the attic, and everything else that we had ever done. I wanted to talk about the fight. I wanted to tell him I was sorry.

But it was too late.

I stopped walking. I stood – just stood – in the rain. It was heavy now, but I didn't care. I didn't even notice.

I took out my phone. I checked to see if I had Joe's number. Drops of rain fell on the screen.

I didn't.

I didn't have his number. That was the worst part. I remembered now, I had got rid of it. I had deleted it. Years ago, after the fight. I remembered telling Sarah that I would never talk to Joe again. I remembered pressing the key, and I saw his name and number go. It was like I had killed him.

That was stupid. I knew that. I didn't kill Joe.

But all those years, I never spoke to him.

My mam walked into her bedroom. She was taking her coat and her scarf off. She saw Joe on the bed. The noise of him landing was still in the room. She saw the dust and the plaster.

'Hi, Mrs Dunne,' said Joe. 'I just dropped in for a chat.'

She looked up at the hole in the ceiling, and saw me looking down.

She started laughing.

I walked home in the rain. There was no one else on the street.

No one.

I was the only man in the city. In the world. That was how I felt.

Chapter Five

I remember opening the front door. It's funny, the things we remember, the little details. But I remember it clearly, putting the key in the lock. It seemed to take more effort. My fingers were freezing and stiff. The key felt too big in my hand. I dropped the key. I had to pick it up again.

I pushed open the door. I was freezing. I wanted to feel the heat.

Sarah was standing in the hall.

'What's wrong?' I said.

It was a stupid question. I knew that when I heard myself say it.

'You were a long time,' she said.

'I lost track of the time,' I said.

'Did you go anywhere?' she asked.

She meant the pub.

'No,' I said. 'I didn't. I just kept walking.'

'Did you meet anyone?' she asked.

'No.'

'Okay.'

It was strange. She was never like this. There

was a time, years ago, when I messed around a bit. I drank too much. I stayed away from the house too often. There had been a bit of trouble with the law. (The law won.) There had been one or two other women – but nothing serious. I had changed. Sarah knew those days were over. It had taken me a long time to get her trust again.

She didn't trust me now. I could see it in her face. I hardly knew her.

'What's wrong?' I asked her again. 'Sarah?'

I moved closer to her.

'Nothing,' she said. 'Sorry.'

She tried to smile.

'It's just so sad,' she said.

'Yes.'

She put her arms around me and hugged me. She was Sarah again, warm and normal. She cried. I put my hand to her face, to wipe away her tears.

But there were no tears.

She stepped back.

'Let's watch some telly,' she said.

'Okay.'

We started to watch *The Killing*. Sarah loved murder, when it came from Denmark or Sweden. I watched it too but, really, I saw nothing.

I wanted to talk about Joe.

'Sarah?' I said.

She put *The Killing* on Pause.

'What?'

'Joe died,' I said.

'What do you mean?' she said. 'I know he died.'

'Why aren't we talking about him?' I asked.

She pointed the remote control at the telly and turned it off.

'Because,' she said. 'It brings back bad memories.'

'I understand,' I said. 'But –'

'What?'

'My memories are not bad,' I said. 'I knew him before you did.'

'That is true,' she said.

She looked at me for a long time. Well, it felt like a long time. Then it was like she woke up.

I have to say this. Sarah was a funny woman. She was full of life. She was sexy, and a bit mad. And the madness made her even sexier. It was nice madness. And she got madder and sexier as she got older. She grinned all the time. She joked. She laughed. She flirted.

This woman I was sitting beside now – it wasn't the same Sarah.

She had the same face, but it was kind of empty. Her eyes were still blue but – dead.

I thought it was because of Joe. It had knocked the life out of her. It had knocked some of the life out of me.

She sat up. It was like she had been pinched. She looked at me. Her eyes were bright again. Her smile made those lovely little creases on her face.

'Let's have a drink,' she said.

'Good idea.'

'Not tea,' she said.

'God, no.'

There was a table near the door, with the bottles on it. She hopped off the sofa and went to the table. She picked up a bottle.

'Empty,' she said.

She picked up another one.

'Bloody empty.'

She looked at me.

'It wasn't me,' I said.

'I know,' she said. 'It was Gavin.'

Gavin was our son. He was twenty-two. He still lived with us. He ate everything in the house and drank everything in the house, but we only saw him about two times a week.

'I'll kill him.' she said. 'He must have had friends in the house. Aha!'

She held up a bottle.

'Happy days,' she said.

'What is it?' I asked.

'Vodka,' she said. 'And there's orange juice in the fridge.'

'Grand,' I said.

'Don't go away,' she said, and she went out to the hall and the kitchen.

I could hear the fridge open.

I heard her shout, 'No!'

I heard her shut the fridge door. She tried to slam it.

She came back in.

'He drank all the orange juice as well,' she said.

He didn't. I did. But I said nothing.

'So,' she said.

She was grinning – the old Sarah.

'What do you want with your vodka, Pat?' she asked. 'Milk or water? Or vinegar?'

I laughed. I had nearly forgotten that I was able to laugh.

'I can go to the shops for juice,' I said. 'It will only take a minute.'

'No!'

Sarah looked scared.

'Stay with me,' she said. 'Please.'

'Okay,' I said.

I sat down. I wanted her to start smiling again.

She sat beside me. Right in beside me.

'We'll pretend we are teenagers,' she said.

She put the vodka bottle up to her lips.

'No need for a glass,' she said.

'Glasses are for old people,' I said.

'I hate old people.'

'Me too.'

She patted my bald head. Then she gave me the bottle.

We talked about Joe while we got through the vodka. I did most of the talking.

I told Sarah about the time me and Joe had climbed into the monkey house at the zoo. I told her about the time we had gone out with twins.

'At least, they told us they were twins,' I said.

'And were they?' she asked.

'No,' I said. 'They were not even sisters. They just said they were.'

'Did they even look like each other?'

'Kind of,' I said. 'Their hair was the same.'

I told her about the time Joe got sick in my school bag, and about the time I got sick in his schoolbag. I told her about the holiday in Spain, when we ended up in Turkey. And about the time we got locked into a pub all night. And the time we got locked into the pub again.

I only told her the good stuff.

We had a great night. I think. We got drunk.

I know. We made love. I think. We made love again. I think, but I'm not sure. But I think.

And I was falling asleep.

And she was staring down at me.

I think.

Chapter Six

I woke the next morning.

She was still staring down at me.

No, she wasn't. I blinked and she was not there. The bedroom was empty, except for me.

The smell came up from the kitchen.

Bacon and eggs.

It was a normal smell. But not on a weekday. I was out of the house very early, by half-six, most mornings. So I had my breakfast, coffee and toast, at work.

What day was it?

I had to think about it.

Thursday.

I looked at my watch. It was nine o'clock. I was late for work, or I was not going at all.

I went downstairs.

'Good morning,' I said.

Sarah looked at me. She was at the cooker and she had her phone up to her ear.

'I know,' she said, to the phone.

She listened to whoever was at the other end. Then she spoke again.

'Yes, that's right,' she said. 'Joe was always like that.'

Joe.

I had not been thinking about Joe. I had nearly forgotten about him. And that made me feel bad.

But I was still hungry.

Sarah was still listening to the phone. She lifted the kettle and showed it to me.

'Yes,' I said. 'Thanks.'

Maybe she wanted me to fill it but I was a bit slow that morning. She put it into the sink and turned on the cold tap. I heard the sound of the kettle filling. She took the kettle from the sink. I heard the click as she turned it on.

'Lungs?' she asked whoever she was talking to.

When I heard that, I knew that Joe had died of cancer.

Joe had been a smoker since we were kids. Me too – I had smoked as well. But I gave them up when I was thirty. Joe gave them up too, but he went back on them, and off them, and on them again, and off them.

And back on them.

There was once, Joe gave up the smokes and went back on them in one day. Twice.

Anyway, the cancer got him.

And I never knew he was sick.

And that made me sick.

But I was still hungry. I felt guilty because I was hungry. But the smell of the bacon was a killer. You can't stay guilty for too long when there is frying bacon in the air.

Joe would not have wanted me to stop eating just because he was dead.

I watched Sarah putting the eggs on the plates, with the toast and the rashers. She did it with one hand while she held the phone to her ear.

My heart was broken but my stomach was groaning.

I thought I heard Joe laughing.

It was strange, but that cheered me up. The idea that Joe was watching me, and listening to me. That he wasn't really dead.

I even looked around, to check that Joe was not there. He wasn't. Of course, he wasn't.

I listened to Sarah on the phone while I messed with sugar in the sugar bowl. I wished she would hurry up. I was starving.

'Oh, God love him,' said Sarah. 'In his sleep? Well, that's good, at least.'

She listened for a while, and looked at me.

'Poor Karen,' she said.

Karen was Joe's wife.

'Eleven,' said Sarah. 'Tomorrow.'

I knew then that was the time of the funeral.

'Sad,' said Sarah, into the phone. 'Sad, sad. Yes, very sad. Bad, shocking. Sad. Bye now, Mary. Bye, bye, bye, bye, bye, bye.'

She put the phone on the kitchen table.

'That Mary one never shuts up,' she said. 'It was cancer.'

'Mary?'

'Joe.'

I nodded.

'The lungs,' said Sarah.

'I heard that bit,' I said. 'Which Mary was it?'

We knew a lot of Marys.

'Mary from the shop,' said Sarah.

'Which one?' I asked.

Two women called Mary worked in the local supermarket, with Sarah.

'Big Hair Mary,' said Sarah.

I knew who she meant.

It seemed strange, and maybe wrong. But I was enjoying myself. My head was a bit sore and my best friend was dead. But Sarah was her normal self. Her hair was a bit mad and she was coming at me with a plate full of food. I was madly in love with her.

'I love you,' I said.

'You love rashers,' she said.

'I love you too,' I said.

'But not as much as the rashers,' she said.

'Nearly as much.'

I took a bite.

'Lovely,' I said. 'Thanks. I'll be late for work.'

'You're not going to work,' said Sarah.

I looked at her. She wasn't eating. She was smiling but there was something wrong about the smile. It was like the different Sarah again.

'How come?' I asked.

'I phoned in,' she said. 'Gerry can do without you for one day.'

It annoyed me, a bit. I did not want to go to work, but I had to. There was just me and Gerry, and we had three different gig posters to print and deliver by the end of the day. There wasn't much money coming in. We were just about hanging on.

'I have to go in,' I said.

I even stood up.

'No.'

It was the way she said it. I froze. She looked at me for a second, maybe two seconds, and spoke.

'Gerry said he can manage without you,' she said.

I looked back at her. More than anything

else, I wanted her to smile. I wanted the old Sarah back.

'Okay,' I said. 'I won't go in.'

And she smiled.

'The funeral is tomorrow.'

I forgot – again. Joe was dead.

'Oh,' I said. 'Okay.'

'We'll go to that.'

'Of course.'

She nodded, and smiled again.

'And the wake,' she said. 'We will go to the wake.'

'The wake?'

'Yes,' said Sarah. 'In the house.'

She meant Joe's house. She meant Joe and Karen's house. And their son, Sam. We used to spend as much time in that house as we did in our own. Sam and our son, Gavin, played together. They grew up together, for a while.

Before the fight.

'Is it tonight?' I asked.

'Yes,' said Sarah.

'God,' I said. 'I don't know, love.'

'We have to,' said Sarah.

'I don't know if I can face Karen,' I said.

'Me too,' said Sarah. 'But –'

'We have to,' I said.

'Yes.'

'Will Joe be there?' I asked her.

She stared at me.

'Joe's dead,' she said. 'Remember?'

'The body,' I said. 'In the coffin, like. Will it – will *he* be there?'

That was when I heard Joe laugh again.

Joe was dead. But in my head he was coming back to life. Too late.

'What's wrong? Sarah asked.

'Nothing,' I said.

'The wake,' she said.

I nodded.

'Okay,' I said. 'We'll go.'

'Now eat your breakfast,' she said.

'Okay – thanks.'

The bacon was cold but cold bacon was better than no bacon. And soggy toast was even nicer than fresh toast.

Sarah hadn't touched her food.

'Are you not eating?' I asked her.

'I'm not really hungry,' she said. 'You can have it.'

She pushed her plate across the table.

I didn't need it.

But I wanted it.

'Thanks.'

I was dreading the night and going to Joe's house. The time would go slower if I kept eating.

Chapter Seven

I have something to get off my chest.

I had a thing with Karen. It was years before, when I was a bit wild. Sarah never knew about it, and Joe did not know about it. It did not last long. It was stupid. It was wonderful.

It ended.

There was no harm done.

No one died. As they say.

Chapter Eight

We walked to Joe's house that night, after dinner.

It was like walking back into the time when I was a child.

Joe and Karen lived in the house where Joe had grown up. I knew every corner, every tree and gate on the way there. Over there was the wall I'd fallen off and broken my arm, when I was ten.

'Joe pushed me,' I told Sarah.

'Good for Joe,' said Sarah.

She held my arm.

Like I said, it was like walking back into my childhood. Except for one thing. There was nobody out. Nobody at all. Just me and Sarah.

'These streets were packed when I was a kid,' I told her.

'Is that right?' she said.

'We played football 'til after dark,' I said. 'The games went on for hours.'

'There are too many cars these days,' said Sarah. 'For street football.'

But there were no cars. There were only parked cars. But no cars passed us. Not one.

I listened. I could not hear a car engine, or a kid shouting. Or a dog barking.

I stopped walking.

Sarah pulled my arm.

'Come on.'

'There's no one out,' I said.

'It's cold,' she said.

That was true. It was very cold. We started to walk fast. Sarah pulled me along, and made me run across the street where I used to live. She laughed when we got to the other side.

We were outside the house where Miss Hayes, the local witch had lived. I pointed to it.

'That one there,' I told Sarah. 'The one with the blue door.'

'Why did you think she was a witch?' Sarah asked.

'Well,' I said. 'She looked like one.'

'What?' said Sarah. 'Did she fly on a broomstick?'

'No,' I said. 'I never saw her do that. But she had long hair.'

'And that made her a witch?'

'It was more than just long,' I said. 'It was kind of mad.'

'So you called her a witch,' said Sarah. 'Just

because she was a bit different.'

I wished now that I had kept my mouth shut.

'She ate a baby once,' I said.

'She did not!' said Sarah.

She stopped walking and looked at me.

'Tell me she didn't,' she said.

'Okay.'

'Okay what?'

'Okay,' I said. 'She didn't eat a baby.'

'I knew you were making it up,' said Sarah.

'Yes,' I said. 'It was more like a toddler.'

'She ate a toddler?'

'Only half of it,' I said. 'He was a big lad. She put the rest of him in the fridge.'

Sarah laughed – and then stopped. We were getting close to Joe's house. We stopped talking. Sarah stopped holding my arm. Her hand dropped, and held my hand. I was going slower now. I wanted the walk to go on for ever. I didn't want to reach the house – the front door – the hall – and Joe.

The street was full of parked cars. The house was going to be full. Although there was still nobody else out on the street.

We got to the gate.

I stopped.

There was a tree in Joe's front garden. It had been there since we were kids. I don't know much about nature. I don't know the names of birds or trees. So I don't know what kind of a tree it was. But I knew that my name was carved into it, and I knew exactly where my name was.

I walked a few steps across the grass and showed it to Sarah.

'Look,' I said.

She followed me, and looked at the letters. It was dark, so she had to bend down to see them. I held my phone beside the letters, so she could read them.

'"Pat",' she read.

'That's me,' I said.

'You were smaller when you did this,' said Sarah.

'Yes,' I said. 'I was only about ten.'

'Why did you do it?' she asked.

Women ask some amazing questions sometimes.

'Because it was there,' I told her. 'And because I had a penknife.'

'Come on,' she said.

She held my hand and we walked the rest of the way, to the front door.

She put her finger on the doorbell.

We could hear people inside. Lots of people.

'Are you ready?' she asked.

'No,' I said.

But I nodded, and Sarah rang the bell.

But the door was already opening in front of us before we heard the bell.

There was a boy of about twenty looking at us. He was looking down at us a bit, because he was so tall. He was tall, and very like Joe.

I did not know what to say.

Sarah squeezed my hand, then she let go of it.

'Hello, Sam,' she said.

We watched the kid's face change. He did not know who we were at first. But then, when Sarah spoke, he remembered us.

'Hi,' he said.

'Hello, Sam,' I said now.

I think he was ten the last time I had seen him, or he had seen me.

'How are you?' I asked.

'Grand,' he said.

It was hard, looking at Sam. I was happy to see him. I was very happy. I had always liked him when he was a little lad. But now, he looked so like his dad. He was so like my best friend, Joe.

He was wearing a black jacket that was too small for him. His white shirt was much too big for him. I wanted to hug him but I still did not know what to say.

Sarah saved the day. She put her arms around the lanky kid and hugged him.

'We're sorry, Sam,' she said.

It was as if he was ten again.

'Thanks, Aunty Sarah,' he said.

Then he stood back and let us into the hall. That was good, because it was cold out there in the garden. I have been bald for a few years now. Cold nights are no fun for bald men.

We were in the hall.

'What now?' I whispered to Sarah.

'Come on,' she said.

Chapter Nine

It was strange walking into the house. I knew it as well as my own. I used to play in the hall and on the stairs with Joe, when we were kids. Later, when I was older, I used to bring my kids here, to play with Joe's kids.

It was like being in my own house.

But it wasn't.

It was like being in a dream. It was like walking through a dream I had been in before. I knew what was coming up but I was still scared.

The house was full. It was packed.

It was full of faces I knew. There were men and women I had not seen in years and men and women I saw every day. There were old faces that had been young the last time I saw them. It was a bit scary, like a scene from a horror film. It was like a house full of very old children.

'Is that Pat Dunne?' asked an old woman.

She grabbed my arm.

'How are you, Mrs Webb?' I said.

'You remember me,' she said.

'I do, yes,' I said.

Remember her? Mrs Webb had been the best-looking mother in Barrytown when I was a teenager. It was a shock to see her now.

'You are looking well,' I told her.

'Ah, now,' she said.

She looked tired after all that chat.

It was sad. But it was funny too, in a way. She was an old lady but I was a bald man with a belly the size of my head. If I was shocked, so was she.

She let go of my arm.

'How is your dad?' she asked.

My dad had been dead for ten years. He had lived beside Mrs Webb for more than forty years.

'He is fine,' I told her.

'Ah, good,' she said.

'Bye bye, Mrs Webb.'

I kept going. But she grabbed me. Her grip was strong, and sore.

'It's not so bad,' she said.

'Okay.'

'You get used to it,' she said.

'Grand.'

She let go of me.

'We'll meet again,' she said.

'Yes.'

'And again and again.'

'Okay.'

'We'll never stop meeting.'

'Fine.'

There was a door to my left. It was open but I did not look in. It was the front room. It was the good room. I knew the coffin would be in there. Joe was in there, in the coffin. I was not ready to look yet.

I kept going. Sarah had stopped, behind me. She was talking to someone. I wanted to wait for her, but I kept going. I kept going past people I used to know.

'Hello,' said someone.

'Hello, Pat,' said someone else. 'Long time, no see.'

'It's great to have you back,' said another.

I smiled and kept going. I walked into the kitchen, alone.

It was even more packed than the rest of the house. It was hot. There was steam on the windows and all the bald heads in the room were glowing.

A tall, fat guy got out of my way.

And I saw Karen.

Do I need to remind you? Karen was Joe's wife. She was Joe's widow now. And I had a fling with her. Back in the day. Before I had the fight with Joe.

And, no, the fight had not been about me

and Karen. As I said before, the fight had been about a horse.

But I am going to be very honest. As I stood in the steamy kitchen, I kind of wished I was still having the fling with Karen. Karen was a fine thing. She was the best-looking widow in the room.

She saw me.

She did not look too happy. But then, her husband was dead and in a box just down the hall. Why would she have looked happy?

I smiled at her. I think I smiled. It was a bit hard to tell. My face was numb and stiff. But I think I smiled. I made the effort.

'Hello, Karen,' I said.

I wished Sarah was with me now. She was better at this kind of thing.

Then I started to cry.

'I'm sorry,' I said.

The room went a bit silent. People were looking, people were listening. People were waiting. They knew the story. They knew all about the fight.

It was as if they had all been standing there, waiting for this moment.

Karen stood in front of me. My nose nearly touched her nose. She was a tall woman and I am not a very tall man. She really was a lovely-looking widow.

She held my hands. She took both of them in her own two hands. She had big hands, for a woman. She had nice, soft, big hands.

'Pat,' she said. 'I'm glad you came.'

'So am I,' I said. 'I just wish –'

'What?' she said.

'I wish I had done this sooner.'

'Ah, well,' she said. 'Joe said the same thing.'

'Did he?'

'Yes.'

'We were stupid,' I said.

'Yes,' she said. 'We were.'

'I mean, me and Joe,' I said.

I could feel myself blushing.

'Yes,' she said. 'That too. But here you are.'

Her hands went around me and we hugged. I kissed the side of her face. Her ear was right there, ready for my words.

And I saw my son looking at me.

My son, Gavin, was standing beside the fridge. He had a can of Heineken in one hand and a girl in the other. And he was looking across at me as I kissed the dead man's wife.

What was he doing there?

Then I remembered. Gavin had spent days in this house when he was a little lad. He had played with Sam. He had called Joe, Uncle Joe. He had called Karen, Aunty Karen.

I let go of Aunty Karen.

I smiled across at Gavin. He smiled back. He was twenty-two and sometimes he did not smile at all. But he did this time and that was nice. I had not seen him in a few days. I could not remember exactly when. We lived in the same house but only saw each other two or three times a week. I was going to go over and chat to him and the girl. I had not seen her before. But Karen patted my shoulder.

'Go in and see Joe,' she said.

Her hand stayed on my shoulder.

I didn't want to. I didn't want to look at Joe in the coffin. But the good-looking widow had told me to do it. I felt a bit evil, but that was okay. I used to feel evil a lot. And it was fine. There were worse ways to feel.

'Okay,' I said.

I looked over at Gavin. The girl with him looked nice. She was pretty but a bit pale. The fake tan was not doing its job.

I shouted across to him.

'I'll be back in a minute!'

Heads turned. People stared at me. I had been too loud. It was a wake, for God sake. There was death in the house.

I was sweating. I needed a drink. But Karen was waiting for me to go back out, to Joe. Her hand gave me a gentle push.

'Go on,' she said. 'He's waiting for you.'

It was a strange thing to say, but I smiled. I kissed her on the cheek again, and turned.

Sarah was right behind me. I nearly walked into her.

'All right?' she asked.

'I was just talking to Karen,' I said.

'So I see,' said Sarah.

I could feel my face going red again.

'I'm going to see Joe,' I told her.

'Good,' she said.

She kissed me on the cheek. I was getting tired of women kissing me on the cheek. It was too dangerous.

I saw now, there was another woman standing beside Sarah.

She was about my age. She wore a suit, like she was coming home from work. Her hair was up on her head and her reading glasses sat on top, like an extra pair of ears. Her eyes were blue and lovely. The rest of her was nearly as lovely as her eyes.

'Do you know Sandra?' Sarah asked me.

'No,' I said.

'Sandra used to live around here,' said Sarah.

Sandra put her hand out.

'Nice to meet you – is it Pat?' she said.

'That's right,' said Sarah. 'Pat.'

I shook her hand. It was a bit cold.

'I'm going to see Joe,' I told Sarah.

'Good,' she said.

'I just got here,' said the other woman, Sandra. 'I need a cup of tea. I'll follow you in.'

'Here goes,' I said to Sarah.

And I walked out of the kitchen.

Chapter Ten

I went out to the hall. It was still packed. The same people were standing in the same places, leaning against the same bit of wall. And the same old woman was blocking the way.

'Is that Pat Dunne?' she said, again.

'How are you, Mrs Webb?'

'You remember me.'

'Oh, I do.'

'It's not so bad,' she said.

'Yes.'

'You get used to it,' she said.

'So you said.'

'We'll meet again,' she said.

'Yes, I know,' I said.

'And again.'

I got past her.

Young Sam was still standing at the front door, in his too-big shirt.

I waved but he didn't wave back.

The good room was to my right. That door was open. There was nobody going in or coming out. I would be alone in there. With Joe. With the body.

I was tempted to keep on walking. I would open the front door and walk out, down the path. I'd walk all the way home. Maybe I'd pop into the pub on the way.

No.

I had to see Joe. I had to pay my respects.

I stepped up to the door. I stepped in.

The room was empty. Except for the coffin. And Joe.

I gasped. I nearly screamed.

'Joe!'

'How's it going?' said Joe.

He was in the coffin, but he was sitting up in it. He didn't look too bad, for a dead man. He probably looked better than I did.

'Joe,' I said, again.

'That's me,' he said.

He sounded exactly like Joe. I mean, it was Joe's voice. But he was supposed to be dead. That was why I was there.

'You are not dead,' I said.

'You look a bit let down,' said Joe.

But he smiled.

'I'm not,' I said. 'It's just –'

'Unusual,' said Joe.

'Yes,' I said. 'Kind of.'

It was more than unusual.

'It's a bit strange,' I said.

There was a dead man talking to me. It was very bloody strange. But there was another strange thing. When Joe smiled, it hit me that he looked no older. He looked the way he had the last time we spoke. The day we had the fight. I was older and I looked older. I knew that. Sarah told me every day. And I saw it in the mirror when I shaved. I was getting older all the time.

But Joe wasn't.

'You look great,' I told him.

He wore a dark blue suit and a black tie. If he had been looking for work, I would have given him the job.

'It's gas,' he said. 'Isn't it?'

'What do you mean?' I asked him.

'Well, here I am,' he said.

He tapped the side of the coffin. He looked a bit daft in it, like it was a little sailboat – with no sail. Or a pram.

'I'll get out and stretch my legs,' he said.

He laughed. And so did I. I was starting to enjoy the news. Joe wasn't dead. I watched him climb out of the coffin. He kind of slid out, legs first, over the side. It was a bit like he was doing the high jump. But he was doing the high jump in a suit and tie. He didn't even grunt.

He was standing right in front of me now. It was great. But I still needed answers.

'What's the story?' I said.

'What do you mean?' he asked.

'Ah, come on, Joe,' I said. 'Your funeral is tomorrow. Your death was in the paper.'

'Oh,' said Joe. 'That?'

'Yes,' I said. 'That.'

'Well,' said Joe. 'Have you any idea how much funerals cost?'

'They're expensive. Are they?'

'Ah, man,' he said. 'You have no idea. They cost a fortune.'

'I thought so,' I said. 'I remember my dad's funeral cost a good bit.'

'It leaves a big hole in your pocket,' said Joe.

'I'd say so,' I said.

'Oh, yeah,' said Joe. 'In fact, it leaves a big hole in *my* pocket.'

Joe's face looked a bit plastic. There was a shine off it that didn't seem right.

'So,' he said. 'I said to myself. Why wait?'

'Sorry, Joe,' I said. 'I'm a bit lost. What do you mean?'

'Why wait 'til I was dead?' said Joe.

'Hang on,' I said.

I stepped back. I didn't mean to, but I could not help it. His face looked so pale and glossy, and what he was saying was so mad.

'What's wrong?' he asked.

'Nothing,' I said. 'Just –'

'What?'

'Are you having your funeral before you die?' I asked him. 'Is that what you are telling me?'

'Exactly,' said Joe.

He tapped the side of the coffin again.

'I paid for this thing,' he said. 'So I might as well enjoy it.'

I began to relax again. What Joe was saying did make sense. A bit. Good coffins cost a lot of money. His face looked normal again. His skin looked like skin, not plastic.

'Do you want to give it a go?' he asked.

'What?'

'The coffin,' he said.

'What?' I said. 'Do you want me to get into it?'

'Only if you want.'

'What's it like?' I asked.

'Not too bad,' said Joe. 'A bit tight.'

I went nearer to the coffin, and looked in.

'Is it padded?' I asked.

Joe stood beside me.

'Only a bit,' he said. 'You would not want to spend too long in there.'

'But –'

'I know,' he said. 'I know. But I'll be dead.'

'But you're not dead now,' I said.

He didn't answer.

'Are you?' I asked him.

He still didn't answer.

'Joe?' I said. 'Are you dead?'

He looked at me. He smiled.

'Well, yes,' he said. 'I am.'

He looked at the door.

'Hang on,' he said. 'There's someone coming.'

He put his hands on the coffin, lifted himself, and slid in. He moved like a kid, easy and quick. He lay on his back. He winked at me, then closed his eyes.

Chapter Eleven

I thought I'd die.

Joe was dead!

That was mad, I know. That was why I was there, in his house. Because Joe was dead. But then, he wasn't dead. And then, he was dead again. He was in the coffin and he looked very dead. But for a while, I had really thought he was alive.

But –

But –

But this was the thought that made my legs start to wobble. He was dead but he was alive. He was alive and dead. My best friend was a zombie. Or something. I wasn't sure what a zombie was. Or how you became a zombie. Was there an exam or a test? All I knew was, Joe was dead and Joe was alive.

Someone had walked into the room.

I didn't look.

'Doesn't he look super?' said the someone.

It was a woman.

I looked behind me. It was the woman from

the kitchen. Her glasses still sat on top of her hair, like an extra pair of ears. Her eyes were still blue and lovely.

She smiled.

'Pat Dunne,' she said.

It took me a while to answer. I was still in shock. I wasn't sure I *was* Pat Dunne.

But then it came back to me. I knew who I was. There was a good looking woman beside me and I wanted to impress her.

'Yes,' I said. 'I'm Pat Dunne.'

So far, so good.

I sucked in my belly. And I thought I heard Joe laugh. I looked, but his eyes were shut.

'You haven't changed,' she said.

I heard that laugh again. But she had not heard it. I could tell that from her face.

'You don't know me,' she said. 'Do you?'

I looked at her carefully. I enjoyed myself.

'No,' I said. 'I give up. No, hang on –'

She laughed.

'Sandra,' she said.

'You're Sandra Nolan,' I said.

'Well done,' she said.

'God,' I said.

'What?'

I didn't know what to say. When me and Joe were kids – when we were teenagers – we had loved Sandra Nolan. We hung around outside her house. We sat on her wall. We waited outside her school when we should have been in our own school. I fancied her so much, I lay awake all night. Thinking of her.

I looked at her now, and I remembered. I had asked her up to dance once. Years ago.

Thirty years ago.

At a dance in the Barrytown United clubhouse.

Chapter Twelve

Joe pushed me.

'Go on,' he said.

'No,' I said. 'She'll say No.'

We were looking across at Sandra Nolan. She was dancing with her friends. They were in a circle. Their handbags and coats were in a pile on the floor and they were dancing around the bags. The hall was hot and the steam was as thick as juice. There was a smell of Brut and football socks.

'Go on,' said Joe. 'A little bird told me she'll say Yes if you ask her.'

'Really?' I said. 'Who?'

'Ah now,' said Joe. 'I have my spies. Just ask her.'

'And she'll say Yes?'

'My spy – '

'Who?'

'Shut up,' said Joe. 'Just trust me. Ask her.'

The DJ was an eejit called Paddy O'Hara who called himself the Night Wolf.

'That was Black Sabbath,' said Paddy the

Night Wolf. 'But *NOW* we'll slow things *DOWN*. Here's Lionel Richie. *Hello*.'

'Now is your chance,' said Joe. 'Go on.'

'I hate this song,' I said.

'Never mind the song,' said Joe. 'Think of the bird.'

He pushed me again, in the back. I slid over the sweat and Fanta and walked the rest of the way. To Sandra Nolan. Her back was to me. Her lovely back, with her lovely hair.

I stopped.

I waited.

I heard Joe's voice.

'Go on!'

I tapped her shoulder.

She turned.

I was blushing. I felt the heat in my face. I tried to smile.

'Do you want to dance?' I asked.

'No,' she said. 'Get lost.'

Chapter Thirteen

Sandra was looking down at Joe. She lifted her hand and wiped her eye.

'He was my first ride,' she said.

'What?'

I wasn't sure I had heard her properly. I *hoped* I hadn't heard her properly.

'My first ride,' she said.

She nodded at Joe in the coffin.

'That man there.'

She looked at me now. Did she expect me to say something?

'It's sad,' she said. 'Isn't it?'

Now I could speak.

'Yes,' I said.

She turned away from the coffin. I looked, and Joe was smiling up at me.

'When did it happen?' I asked her.

I was still looking at Joe.

'Years ago,' she said. 'Behind the Barrytown United clubhouse.'

'At the dance?'

'Yes,' she said. 'Do you remember that dance?'

'I do,' I said. 'Yes.'

Joe was still smiling. I wanted to kill him. But he was dead already. Or half dead, or something.

She turned and looked in at Joe. His eyes were shut, but I hadn't seen him close them. She looked around, to see if anyone was coming into the room. But it was just us. Me, her – and Joe.

'It's a bit creepy,' she said. 'You know. My first lover is dead.'

She shivered. She made herself shiver. Her glasses slid off her head, past her nose. She caught them and put them back up on her head.

'It must be strange,' I said.

'A bit,' she said. 'But mostly just sad.'

I was afraid of the answer I was going to hear, but I had to ask the question.

'Was he any good?'

'No,' she said. 'God love him. He was done in five seconds.'

Joe's eyes popped open, then closed.

'I didn't know what the fuss was all about for years,' she said.

'Yes,' I said. 'I know what you mean.'

I had no idea why I said that. Did she think now that I had had sex with Joe as well? I had to say something else – quick.

'Do you think it will rain?' I asked.

No, I didn't. I'm not that bad. Anyway, there is no point in asking that question in Ireland. The answer is always Yes.

'I asked you up for a dance once,' I said. 'Do you remember?'

'No,' she said. 'Did you, really?'

'Yeah,' I said. 'But you said No.'

She put her hand to her head and slid her reading glasses down to her nose. She looked at me, over the glasses.

'No,' she said. 'I didn't.'

She put the glasses back up on her head.

'Ah, well,' she said.

I felt like she had seen right through my clothes. And right through my skin and flesh. Into the hollow place where my heart used to be, before it fell down through my body, onto the floor. I felt empty and old and fat but – do you know what? I didn't really care. It was kind of nice. I was miserable, but kind of happy too.

I smiled at her.

She smiled back.

'I have to go,' she said. 'My book club is on tonight.'

She looked in at Joe one more time. His eyes were closed. He was looking very dead.

'Bye, Joe,' she whispered.

'What's the book?' I asked her.

'What?'

'The book club,' I said. 'What book did you read?'

'I didn't,' she said. 'I never read the book. I just go for the crack. A few drinks and a laugh.'

She stepped back from the coffin.

'Anyway,' she said. 'Bye, Pat.'

She leaned up and kissed me on the cheek. Did her tongue kind of lick my cheek?

I wasn't sure. But I wanted to lick hers.

'You went to Saint Joseph's school,' said Sandra. 'You played for Barrytown United. You wore a blue shirt that you looked great in. With a little bit of chest hair sticking out. You used to hang around outside the shops. You blew smoke rings when we passed by. They were always perfect. They always looked like they were going to come down over our heads.'

She was looking right at me.

'Your hair dropped over your eyes,' she said. 'I always wanted to push it back up. I wanted to put my fingers through your hair.'

She lifted her hand. She was going to put her hand – her fingers – on my head.

She stopped. Her hand dropped.

She smiled.

'Take care of yourself,' she said.

I watched her walk out of the room. Her heels

clicked across the floor. My wife and son were in the house, my best friend was in a coffin beside me. But, still, I nearly called after her.

'Do you want to go for a drink?'

I nearly did.

But I didn't.

Then I did.

'Do you want to go for a drink?' I said. 'Eh – some time.'

She stopped at the door and looked at me again. She stared at me for three long seconds.

'I don't think that would be wise,' she said. 'Do you?'

She lifted her hand and showed me her wedding ring.

'No,' I said. 'I don't think it would be wise.'

I was loving this. It was the new me. It was the old me. I was Pat Dunne, the Sex Machine. Even my voice sounded different. It was deeper.

'But,' I said. 'But do we always have to be wise, Donna?'

'My name is Sandra,' she said.

The old me would have given up. But I was Pat the Sex Machine.

I took my phone out of my pocket.

'What's your number?' I said. 'I'll phone you in a few days.'

She looked at me, then started speaking.

'0 – 8 – 7 – 6 – 2 – 3 – 3 –'

It was amazing. Sandra Nolan gave me her phone number.

No.

She didn't.

I didn't even ask her. I wanted to. I wanted to. I really, really wanted to.

She was gone. I heard the front door open, and close.

Joe was sitting up in the coffin.

'Why didn't you ask her?' he said.

'Oh, look,' I said. 'It's Five Seconds Joe. Back from the dead. Are you able to read my thoughts as well?'

'Why didn't you ask her?' he said again.

'Can you read my thoughts?' I asked him again.

'No, I can't,' he said. 'But I know that I wanted to ask her.'

'Why didn't you?' I asked.

He patted the coffin.

'I'm busy,' he said. 'I already have a gig.'

'You only lasted five seconds,' I said.

'That was five more than you,' he said. 'Anyway, it was seven seconds. At least. She is still a fine thing, isn't she?'

'Sandra?'

'Sandra.'

'Yes.'

'Oh, yes.'

'She is.'

'Oh, she is.'

'Do the dead think about sex?' I asked him.

'That never stops,' said Joe. 'So, why didn't you ask her to go for a drink?'

'I don't know,' I said. 'I wanted to.'

I had not spoken like this in years. To anybody. Even myself. There was something about being with Joe. Alive or dead. Alive *and* dead. I felt I was a little bit dead myself. And free.

'It's not too late,' he said.

'It is,' I said. 'She's gone.'

'She's a woman,' said Joe. 'It will take her ages to go.'

'I heard the front door,' I told him.

'How do you know that was her?' he said.

I ran out to the hall.

I didn't run. But I walked very fast.

Chapter Fourteen

The hall was still the same. The same people – in the same places. The front door was still shut. Young Sam still stood beside it.

Mrs Webb blocked my way.

'Is that Pat Dunne?' she said.

I said nothing. I looked around. They looked back at me, waiting.

'Is that Pat Dunne?'

'How are you, Mrs Webb?'

'You remember me.'

'Yeah.'

'It's not so bad,' she said.

'I know.'

'You get used to it.'

'That's right.'

'We'll meet again,' she said.

'We will.'

I had not seen her move, or shift. But I was able to get past her.

I went the rest of the way to the kitchen door. I stopped, and looked back. No one had moved. They were talking but I could hear no words.

I wanted to go back to Joe. I felt better with him. I felt more safe.

But I walked into the kitchen. It was still packed in there, and hot.

A tall, fat guy got out of my way.

And I saw Karen.

There was no sign of Sandra Nolan.

Or Sarah.

My wife.

Karen saw me.

I kept walking towards her.

'He looks great,' I said.

She stared at me.

I wished Sarah was with me now. She was better at this kind of thing.

Karen took both of my hands in hers.

'Pat,' she said. 'I'm glad you came.'

'You said that already – ' I said, and stopped.

She was upset. I saw that now. She was putting on a brave face. But she was in a bad way. She did not remember that we had already met.

'I wish I had done this sooner,' I said.

'Ah, well,' she said. 'Joe said the same thing.'

'Yes,' I said. 'We were stupid.'

We hugged. I kissed the side of her face. A bit closer to her mouth this time. I left my lips there.

And I saw Gavin looking at me. He was still

standing beside the fridge, with his can and his girl.

'I'll go in and see Joe,' I told Karen.

I turned, and Sarah was right behind me. I nearly walked into her.

'Sarah,' I said.

'All right?' she asked.

'I was just talking to Sandra,' I said.

'Who?'

'I mean, Karen. I was just talking to Karen.'

'So I see,' said Sarah.

She kissed me on the cheek.

I saw now, Sandra Nolan was standing there.

'Do you know Sandra?' Sarah asked me.

What was going on?

'No,' I said.

'Sandra used to live around here,' said Sarah.

Sandra put her hand out.

'Nice to meet you – is it Pat?' she said.

'That's right,' said Sarah. 'Pat.'

'I'm going to see Joe,' I told Sarah.

I legged it, into the hall.

'Is that Pat Dunne?'

'How are you, Mrs Webb?'

'You remember me.'

'Yes.'

'It's not so bad.'

'Spot on.'

'You get used to it.'
'Yeah, yeah.'
'We'll meet again.'
'Yeah.'

Chapter Fifteen

I slid into the front room. Joe was climbing back into the coffin.

'Give me a hand here,' he said.

He did not look so dead now. He looked like a middle-aged man trying to climb up onto a wall. But before I got to him, he lifted himself, and slid in.

He was face down in the coffin. He grunted, and turned. He looked up at me.

'How did it go?' he asked. 'Was she there?'

'Sandra Nolan?'

'Yes,' he said. 'Sandra Nolan.'

'She was there,' I said. 'But it was strange.'

'Was Karen there?'

'Your wife?'

I felt my face burn.

'Yes,' said Joe. 'My wife.'

'She was with Sarah,' I said.

He looked at me. Then he grunted, and sat up in the coffin.

'What's gone wrong with you?' he asked.

'What do you mean?' I said. 'I don't understand.'

'Do you not even remember?'

'Remember what?'

'You,' he said. 'You used to be God's gift to women.'

'Was I?'

'Yes,' he said. 'God, man. Is your memory gone?'

'It must be,' I said.

'Think, for God's sake. Think.'

It was like the word 'Think' opened up my head. I began to remember.

Chapter Sixteen

'That was Black Sabbath,' said Paddy the Night Wolf. 'But *NOW* we'll slow things *DOWN*. Here's Lionel Richie, with *Hello*.'

'Now is your chance,' said Joe. 'Go on.'

'I hate this song,' I said.

'Never mind the song,' said Joe. 'Think of the bird.'

He pushed me again, in the back. I slid over the sweat and spilt Fanta and walked the rest of the way.

Sandra Nolan had her back to me.

I stopped.

I waited.

I heard Joe's voice.

'Go on!'

I tapped her shoulder.

She turned.

I felt the heat in my face. I tried to smile.

'Do you want to dance?' I asked.

She looked like she was going to say No. I could see it in her face.

But I didn't give her the chance.

I don't know how I did what I did next. It just seemed natural. There was no way I was going back across to Joe. He'd be waiting there, laughing at me.

I was calm. I was cool. I really was. But this was the first time I knew I could be like that. I could be that way whenever I wanted to be.

There was another girl standing beside Sandra Nolan.

'Do you want to dance?' I asked her.

I didn't even look at her properly. I smiled, and I moved a little closer to her – just a little. I saw her nod her head. Her hair slid in front of her face. She flicked it back, and I saw that she was kind of lovely.

She put her hands on my shoulders. I put my hands on her waist. God, that was brilliant. And we went slowly round and round as Lionel Richie kept singing 'Hello' to the blind girl in the video. By the time Lionel said 'Goodbye', we were kissing. I didn't even know her name.

I didn't look over at Joe. I didn't care about Joe.

George Michael started singing *Careless Whisper*.

The girl took her mouth away from my mouth.

'I love this one,' she said.

'Yes,' I said. 'It's brilliant.'

I didn't think it was brilliant at all. It was crap. But it didn't matter. The mood was more important than the truth. I didn't know how I knew that. But I did.

We kissed again. We pressed against each other. We nearly fell over.

'Oops,' she said.

We laughed into each other's mouths.

'What's your name?' I asked her.

'Donna,' she said. 'What's yours?'

George Michael gave up and Barry White, the man himself, filled the hall with his growl. *Don't GO changing.*

'I'm Barry,' I told her.

'Barry White?'

'That's me,' I said.

She laughed.

'You're a bit mad,' she said.

'Thanks,' I said.

'I know your real name, anyway,' she said. 'You're Pat Dunne.'

'Only on my days off,' I said.

She laughed.

'It's hot in here, isn't it, Donna?' I said.

'Will we go outside?'

'Good idea,' I said.

We held hands and I led the way. I could see the steam and the cigarette smoke rushing to the open door.

We stepped outside.

Chapter Seventeen

Did I remember all that?

Had it really happened?

I took a deep breath. Joe was looking at me.

Yes, it had happened. I could feel it in my lungs. In the centre of my body. I had once been that boy, and I had walked out of the hall with a girl called Donna. We had walked into the night. We had walked behind a hut. The rest is private. But I will tell you one thing. It lasted longer than five seconds. Even seven.

I looked at Joe. He was lying back in his coffin, looking up at me.

'Tell me if I'm wrong,' I said.

'Go on.'

'I was asking Sandra Nolan up to dance. But I thought she was going to say No. So I asked her friend, Donna . And Sandra got so angry at Donna –'

'A nice girl,' said Joe.

'A very nice girl,' I said. 'Sandra was so angry at Donna and at me. Because, really, she fancied *me*. She used to talk about me with Donna. But now Donna was kissing me. And Sandra was so angry, she looked around and she saw you. You got off with Sandra because she wanted to get off with me. She wanted to make me jealous. Am I right?'

Joe nodded.

'Yes,' he said. 'And it makes me want to die.'

'You are dead, Joe.'

'Well,' said Joe. 'You know what I mean. Watch out.'

He slid down into the coffin and shut his eyes.

Someone had walked into the room.

I didn't look.

'Doesn't he look super?' said the someone.

It was Sandra Nolan.

'You're back,' I said.

I tried not to sound too happy.

Her hair was still up on her head and her reading glasses still sat on top. Her eyes were still blue and still lovely.

She smiled.

'It's Pat Dunne,' she said. 'Isn't it?'

It took me a while to answer. What was going on?

'Yes,' I said. 'It's me.'

And I thought I heard Joe laugh. I looked, but his eyes were shut.

'You haven't changed,' she said.

I heard that laugh again. I wanted to lean into the coffin and hit him. I wanted to put my fist through him. It wasn't funny. There was nothing funny about this.

'You don't know me,' she said. 'Do you?'

I looked at her carefully.

I didn't understand what was going on. Was she flirting with me?

'I give up,' I said. 'No, hang on –'

She laughed.

'You're Sandra Nolan,' I said.

'Well done,' she said.

'You have not changed a bit,' I said.

'Go on out of that,' she said.

She put her hand to her hair.

'I'm a mess,' she said.

She looked down at Joe in the coffin.

'He was your first ride,' I told her.

She didn't seem to hear me. She let her breath out slowly.

She looked at me.

'He was my first ride,' she said.

She nodded at Joe in the coffin.

'That man there.'

Did she expect me to say something?

'It's sad,' she said. 'Isn't it?'

I said nothing.

I looked, and Joe was smiling up at me, just like the last time. Exactly like the last time.

'Behind the clubhouse,' I said.

I was still looking at Joe.

'Years ago,' she said.

Again, it was like she did not hear me – or care.

'Behind the Barrytown United clubhouse,' she said.

'At the dance.'

'Yes,' she said. 'Do you remember that dance?'

'I do,' I said. 'Yes.'

Joe was still smiling. I still wanted to kill him. He was dead already. But I wasn't so sure about that. I wasn't sure about anything.

I was angry. I knew that much.

'It's a bit creepy,' she said. 'You know. My first lover is dead.'

She shivered. Her glasses slid off her head, past her nose.

'It must be strange,' I said.

'A bit,' she said. 'But mostly just sad.'

'Was he any good?'

'No,' she said. 'God love him. He was done in five seconds.'

Joe's eyes popped open, then closed.

'He said seven,' I told her.

Again, it was like I had not spoken.

'I didn't know what the fuss was all about for years,' she said.

'I nearly asked you up to dance once,' I said.

'No,' she said. 'Did you, really?'

'Yeah,' I said. 'But I asked your friend, Donna, instead.'

She put her hand to her head and slid her reading glasses down to her nose. She looked at me, over the glasses.

'Ah, well,' she said.

She put the glasses back up on her head.

'I have to go,' she said. 'My book club is on tonight.'

She looked in at Joe one more time.

'Bye, Joe,' she whispered.

'I bet you didn't read it,' I said.

'What?'

'The book club,' I said. 'I bet you didn't read the book.'

'I didn't,' she said. 'I never read the book. I just go for the crack. A few drinks and a laugh.'

She stepped back from the coffin.

'Anyway,' she said. 'Bye, Pat.'

She leaned up and kissed me on the cheek. I moved, so I kissed her on the lips.

She stepped back. She got away from me.

'You went to Saint Joseph's school,' she said. 'You played for Barrytown United. You wore a blue shirt that you looked great in. With a little bit of chest hair sticking out. You used to hang around outside the shops. Your hair dropped over your eyes. I always wanted to push it back up. I wanted to put my fingers through your hair.'

She lifted her hand.

She stopped. Her hand dropped.

She smiled.

'Take care of yourself,' she said.

I watched her walk out of the room. Her heels clicked across the floor.

She was gone.

I leaned in and grabbed Joe.

'What's going on, you prick?'

I could feel him laughing before I heard him. My hands were close to his neck but he kept laughing.

'Come on,' I said.

I tried to pull him out of the coffin. I looked behind me. There was nobody. I pulled his jacket. But he was too heavy. I could not budge him.

I let go of him. He stopped laughing.

'What's going on, Joe?' I said.

He looked up at me. He was not smiling.

'You'll get used to it,' he said.

'To what?'

'Death.'

'What?!'

'It's all ahead of you.'

I poked his chest with a finger.

'Listen,' I said. 'I came here tonight to say goodbye. To pay my respects.'

'Yes,' he said. 'And you ended up talking to the dead man.'

'Yes,' I said.

'Is it all a dream?' said Joe. 'That's what you are thinking.'

'Kind of.'

'Come here,' he said.

I leaned down, closer to Joe.

'What?'

He grabbed my ear, and pulled.

'Does that answer your question?' he said.

'Let go!'

'Is it a dream?' he said.

'Let go!'

His face was right up against mine. I could feel his breath. I could smell it too. Death didn't smell good.

He let go of my ear.

I stood up, away from him.

'That wasn't a dream,' he said 'Was it?'

'No.'

'The pain was real,' he said.

I nodded.

'But you're still dead,' he said.

'What?!'

'Stop saying "What",' said Joe. 'Just bloody listen. Sorry I pulled your ear, by the way.'

'That's okay,' I said. 'No problem.'

When we were kids, we hit each other all the time. We kicked, we thumped, we spat. We laughed at it. We pulled each other's ears. We battered each other. It was all part of boys being friends.

I wasn't a boy now. If I'd heard Joe right, I was a dead man.

But I wasn't dead. How could I be? My sore ear proved it. I had eaten my dinner before I came here. I had made love to my wife the night before. I had got drunk. I had gone for a walk in the rain. I had come home from work to find out that Joe had died. I had washed my hands – I remembered that. Washing the ink off my fingers. I had been at work before I came home. I had been stuck in traffic on my way home.

I had walked here tonight. I had held Sarah's hand. I had crossed the road. I had seen my name cut into the tree.

I wasn't dead.

But the question was – was Joe?

Was Joe dead?

'Yes,' he said. 'I am.'

I had not asked him the question. I had not opened my mouth.

'And so are you.'

I looked at him.

'Welcome to the club,' he said. 'Hop in.'

I backed away. I turned and ran to the door.

Chapter Eighteen

The hall was still the same.

'Oh, God,' I said.

The same people stood in the same places. Young Sam still stood at the front door.

'Oh, God.'

'Is that Pat Dunne?'

I said nothing. They looked at me, waiting.

'Is that Pat Dunne?' she said.

'How are you, Mrs Webb?'

'You remember me.'

I said nothing.

'It's not so bad,' she said. 'You get used to it.'

I ran back in to Joe. He wasn't sitting up. I had to go all the way over to the coffin to see him.

He wasn't in it.

A hand grabbed my shoulder.

'Boo!'

It was Joe, behind me. But it didn't make me jump. I felt no shock.

'That's the worst part,' said Joe.

'What?'

'You don't really feel anything any more.'

I hit him.

'I do feel something,' I said. 'I'm angry.'

'That's okay,' he said. 'You'll get over that.'

He was rubbing his shoulder, where I had hit him.

'Did that hurt?' I asked.

'No.'

'Why are you rubbing it?'

'Habit,' he said.

I felt my ear, where he had grabbed it.

'It was sore,' I said.

'It's like a memory,' he said. 'Like feeling a leg that has been cut off.'

'Joe,' I said. 'Please. Tell me what's going on.'

'It's simple,' he said. 'You died.'

'When?'

'A good while ago,' he said. 'It doesn't matter.'

'When?!'

'Years,' he said. 'Time doesn't matter any more.'

'Years?!'

'Stop shouting,' said Joe. 'It will not change anything.'

He waved a hand around.

'This is your afterlife,' he said.

'Hang on now,' I said. 'Your house is the afterlife?'

'No,' said Joe. 'It's *your* afterlife.'

'How did that happen?'

'Ah well,' said Joe. 'That's the story.'

Chapter Nineteen

There was so much to take in. The room was full of chairs but I didn't want to sit down. I wanted to run. I wanted to get Sarah and go.

I was dead.

That was mad. There was no way I was dead. I had gone to the toilet a minute before I had left my house. Did dead people go to the toilet? I didn't think so. No. Dead people did not go to the toilet.

'I went to the toilet,' I told Joe.

'What?' said Joe. 'Now?'

'No.'

'Listen, Pat' said Joe. 'The time has come to take this in. You are dead.'

'But –'

'Shut up and listen,' said Joe. 'You died.'

'How?'

'Car crash.'

'I was never in a car crash,' I said.

'You died,' said Joe. 'So you don't remember.'

'Was I alone in the car?' I asked.

I asked the question but I didn't want to hear the answer.

'No,' said Joe. 'You weren't.'

'Who was with me?' I asked.

'Who did you see in the kitchen?' said Joe.

I thought back to Joe's kitchen. The women had been there, and other people I knew. And over at the fridge –

'Gavin?' I said.

Joe nodded.

I wanted to vomit. I wanted to wake up. I wanted everything to be normal again.

Joe was still there. He looked quite happy.

'I'm going to the kitchen,' I said. 'To see Gavin.'

'Okay,' said Joe. 'But you will be back. Why not listen to me now, then go?'

'Go on,' I said.

'Well,' said Joe. 'There is no Heaven. That's the bad news.'

I stood there and let him talk.

'And there is no Hell,' said Joe. 'That's the good news.'

'What is this then?' I asked.

'Well, it's not Hell,' said Joe.

He pointed at the wall.

'I put up that wallpaper,' he said. 'And the devil didn't pay for it. I did.'

The paper was blue and pink.

'It looks like the devil paid for it,' I said. 'I always hated it.'

'Ha ha,' said Joe. 'You are gas. But here is a hint. Do you remember when we had the fight?'

'About the horse,' I said.

Me and Joe had bought a horse, back in the days of the boom, when we had a bit of money. It only ran one race and it came last.

'Forget the horse,' said Joe. 'The fight was never about a horse.'

'It was.'

'Forget about the bloody horse,' said Joe. 'I never cared about the horse. I don't even remember the name of the stupid horse.'

'Safe Bet.'

'What a name for a horse with one lung,' said Joe. 'Anyway. Do you remember where we were?'

'When we had the fight?'

'Yes.'

'Here,' I said. 'In here.'

'That's right,' said Joe. 'Right in here. Was this wallpaper here then?'

I looked at it again.

I tried to remember.

'I got rid of the paper,' said Joe. 'And I painted the walls white. Remember?'

I did. I remembered.

I nodded.

'Yes,' I said.

'Good man,' said Joe. 'So the walls were white when we had the fight. But do you know when you saw this paper last?'

'No,' I said. 'Years ago.'

'Will I tell you, Pat?' said Joe.

I tried to sound calm, as if I didn't care.

'Okay,' I said. 'Fire away.'

'When you came in here with my wife,' said Joe.

'I never –'

'Don't even start,' said Joe. 'Shut your mouth and hear me tell you.'

He was smiling now. And he looked a bit evil. He was enjoying it.

'You came in here,' he said. 'The two of you. And you had sex over there.'

He nodded at the sofa.

'And here.'

He tapped the floor with his foot.

'And while you were at it,' he said, 'you laughed at me.'

'No.'

'No?'

'No,' I said. 'We didn't laugh at you.'

'Ah well,' said Joe. 'I always thought you did.'

'You knew,' I said.

'Yes, I did,' said Joe. 'Of course, I knew.'

'How did you know?'

'Don't be stupid, Pat,' he said. 'It's too late for that. I had eyes. I saw you looking at each other. I *knew*.'

'I'm sorry, Joe,' I said.

'Ah, thanks,' said Joe. 'But I don't care if you are sorry.'

'Why did you let it happen?' I asked.

I looked at Joe's face. A tear rolled from his eye, down his cheek.

Dead men cried.

'I loved her,' he said.

Chapter Twenty

I remembered.

I parked my car on the next street and I walked the rest of the way. I knew Joe was working late. I knew young Sam was at football.

I rang the bell.

Karen opened the door, and stood back. I walked into the hall and shut the door with my foot.

We kissed. It was the first time we had kissed. But we had wanted to – for years. We moved to the front room as we kissed and touched each other. We fell on the sofa. We knocked heads. We laughed.

We dressed quickly when it was over.

We listened for Joe's car.

'We can't do this again,' said Karen.

'Okay,' I said.

But we did.

Chapter Twenty-one

'So,' said Joe. 'This is your afterlife.'

I didn't get it.

'I don't understand,' I said.

'You make your own afterlife,' said Joe.

'What?' I said. 'Like we buy it in IKEA?'

'It's too late for jokes, Pat,' said Joe. 'They don't work here.'

'What do you mean by "here"?'

'Here,' said Joe.

He tapped the floor again.

'This is where you are going to stay,' he said. 'For ever.'

'But I walked here,' I said.

I had been at home. I had walked here after dinner, with Sarah. I could still feel the food in my stomach. We had walked into the house. Sarah was in the kitchen. With Gavin.

'I can walk out,' I said.

Joe nodded.

'I can go any time I want,' I said.

Joe nodded.

'You died two years after me,' he said.

'But you only died a few days ago,' I said.

'You died two years after me,' he said again.

It was all mad but I was starting to believe him.

'We die,' he said, 'and we have our own afterlife. I have mine and you have yours.'

'But you're here, in mine,' I said.

'Not really,' he said. 'I'm in my own one.'

'What is it like?'

'A lot better than your one.'

'Am I in it?'

'No,' he said. 'But Sarah is.'

'Is Sarah dead too?'

He nodded.

'She was in the car?'

He nodded.

'Was I driving?'

He nodded.

I waited. I spoke.

'Was I drinking?'

He nodded.

'Your afterlife is made up of the things you felt bad about,' said Joe. 'The bad things you did, the people you hurt.'

'So I can say sorry?' I asked.

'No,' said Joe. 'No. It does not work that way.'

'Mrs Webb,' I said. 'Out in the hall. What did I ever do to hurt her?'

'You don't remember?'

'No.'

'She will tell you,' he said. 'Just like I told you.'

'And that's it?'

'No,' said Joe. 'It will go on and on.'

I looked around me. It was just a room. A *real* room. A room with walls and a window. And a door.

I was being fooled. I was in a dream. It was like I was underwater. I just had to push and I would get to the air. And wake up.

I pushed Joe away from me. I turned and ran to the door.

Mrs Webb was waiting for me.

'Is that Pat Dunne?'

Young Sam was standing at the door. The others were standing there, looking at me, waiting. Why didn't they move? Why didn't they go home?

'Is that Pat Dunne?' she said again.

'What did I ever do to you?' I asked her.

'Is that Pat Dunne?'

God, it was boring – and terrible.

'How are you, Mrs Webb?'

'You remember me,' she said.

'I do, yeah.'

'It's not so bad,' she said. 'You get used to it.'

No more. I was getting out of here. I'd get Sarah and Gavin, and go.

I went to the kitchen door.

It was a dream, but I knew I had to find Sarah and Gavin before I could wake up.

I was at the kitchen door. Nothing had changed. Gavin was still standing at the fridge. But that proved nothing. He was always at the fridge – or in the fridge.

The girl was still by his side. She still looked nice.

Who was she? Had she been in the car when I crashed it?

There had been no crash. I was still alive, just stuck in a dream.

I saw Karen now. She did not look too happy. But then, her husband was dead and in a box just down the hall.

I stopped.

It was happening again. All over again. The same thing.

I would let it happen, until I got to Sarah. Then I'd escape.

I smiled at Karen. I think I smiled.

'Hello, Karen,' I said.

I wished Sarah was with me now. She was better at this kind of thing.

I shook myself. This was all a game. I would wake up soon.

I looked at Karen.

Then I started to cry.

'I'm sorry,' I said.

The room went a bit silent. People were looking, and listening. People were waiting. They were people I knew. It was like they had all been standing there, waiting for this moment.

Karen stood in front of me.

She held my hands.

'Pat,' she said. 'I'm glad you came.'

'For God's sake, Karen –'

'Pat, I'm glad you came.'

I knew what I had to say.

'So am I,' I said. 'I just wish –'

'What?' she said.

'I wish I had done this sooner.'

'Ah, well,' she said. 'Joe said the same thing.'

I played along.

'Did he?' I said.

'Yes.'

'We were stupid,' I said.

'Yes,' she said. 'We were.'

'I meant me and Joe,' I said.

'Yes,' she said. 'That too. But here you are.'

Her hands went around me and we hugged. I kissed the side of her face. Her ear was right there, ready for my words.

And I saw my son looking at me.

My son, Gavin, was standing beside the fridge.

But I had seen Gavin already. It was a dream – I remembered. I wasn't going to let it happen all over again.

I whispered into Karen's ear.

'I know what's going on,' I said.

She lifted her hand. She patted my shoulder.

'Go in and see Joe,' she said.

I still held on to her.

'I know what's going on, Karen,' I said.

'Go in and see Joe,' she said.

I was going to shock her. I was going to say something really bad.

I put my mouth to her ear.

Then I saw my son, Gavin, over at the fridge. What was he doing there?

Then I remembered. Gavin had spent days in this house when he was a little lad. He had played with Sam. He had called Joe, Uncle Joe. He had called Karen, Aunty Karen.

I let go of Karen.

I smiled across at Gavin. He smiled back. I was going to go over and chat to him and the girl he was with. Who was she? I hadn't seen her before.

Karen patted my shoulder.

'Go in and see Joe,' she said.

Her hand stayed on my shoulder.

'Okay,' I said.

I looked over at Gavin.

I shouted across to him.

'I'll be back in a minute!'

The words felt strange and dry, like I had used them before. I *had* used them before.

'Will this go on for ever?' I asked Karen.

'Go in and see Joe,' she said.

And she gave me a gentle push.

'Go on,' she said. 'He's waiting for you.'

I smiled. I kissed her on the cheek again, and turned.

Sarah was right behind me. I nearly walked into her.

'All right?' she asked.

'I was just talking to Karen,' I said.

'So I see,' said Sarah.

I could feel my face going red.

'I was only talking to her,' I said.

'So I see,' she said.

'It was only once,' I said. 'Sarah, I'm sorry. It meant nothing. It was just a fling.'

She looked at me. She was waiting for me to say the right thing.

'I'm going to see Joe,' I told her.

'Good,' she said.

I kept falling in and out of the story. That was what it felt like. I remembered it was a dream. I forgot it was a dream. I knew I had to do something.

I had to grab Sarah, and escape. Then I'd wake up.

I knew I had to do something.

I stood in front of Sarah.

I knew I had to do something.

Then the woman. Sandra. She was standing beside Sarah.

The glasses were still on top of her head.

'Do you know Sandra?' Sarah asked me.

I looked at Sarah.

'Sarah, come on. Let's go.'

'Sandra used to live around here,' said Sarah.

Sandra put her hand out.

'Nice to meet you – is it Pat?'

I looked around.

Karen was looking. Gavin was looking. Sarah was looking. Sandra was looking.

I grabbed Sarah's arm.

'Come on, Sarah,' I said.

She said nothing. She didn't look at my hand on her arm.

'Sarah,' I said. 'Come on. We can get out now.'

I pulled her arm. She didn't move. It was like she was stuck to the floor.

I looked at her.

'Sarah?'

She just looked back. She said nothing. She smiled. But it wasn't a real smile.

Everyone in the kitchen was looking at me. But they seemed closer. The kitchen was smaller.

I let go of Sarah. I pushed past people. I got to the door. I was in the hall.

'Is that Pat Dunne?'

I pushed past Mrs Webb.

'Is that Pat Dunne?'

If I got out of the house, I'd wake up. Sarah and Gavin would be with me again. Life would be back to normal.

I went past the room where the coffin was. I didn't look in. I heard Joe laugh. I kept going.

I was at the front door.

Sam stood in front of me.

'I have to go,' I told him.

He said nothing. He just stood there. He was a big kid but I pushed him aside.

I grabbed the handle.

I heard Joe laugh.

The door wouldn't open. It was stiff, like it hadn't been opened in years.

Sam stood in front of me. I pushed him again.

'Is that Pat Dunne?'

I lifted my elbow and hit the door glass, hard. It cracked. I hit it again. I stepped back and kicked with my heel.

'Is that Pat Dunne?'

I heard Joe laugh.

The glass fell out, bit by bit. I kicked, I kicked. I kicked until there was space for me to climb out. I cut my hand. I didn't care. I felt the cold air on my face. Glass cut the top of my head. I kept going.

I was out.

I was in the garden.

It was cold and I was safe. I was back in the real world. I didn't look back.

I heard no more laughing.

I ran.

I tried to run all the way. But I wasn't fit. I was real. I was a middle-aged man. It was raining. The rain was real. My breath was real. I walked as fast as I could. I was nearly home. I was cold.

I turned the corner of our street.

I got to the house, up the drive. I took the keys from my pocket. My fingers were freezing and stiff. The door key felt too big in my hand. I dropped the key. I had to pick it up again.

I pushed open the door. I wanted to feel the heat.

I was home now. I was awake. I was safe.

I turned on the hall light.

'Pat!'

Sarah was standing there.

She looked scared, like she had just seen a mouse or something.

'What's wrong?' I said.
She was holding her mobile phone.
'It's Joe,' she said.
'Joe who?' I asked.
She shouted at me.
'Joe!'
She looked pale. Her hands were shaking.
I understood now.
'My Joe?' I said.
She nodded.
'Oh, God,' I said. 'What happened?'
'He's –'
'Dead?'
'Yes,' she said. 'Pat, I'm so sorry.'
She started to cry. And so did I.

Quick Reads

Books in the Series

Available in paperback, ebook and from your local library

Amy's Diary	Maureen Lee
Beyond the Bounty	Tony Parsons
Bloody Valentine	James Patterson
Blackout	Emily Barr
Chickenfeed	Minette Walters
Cleanskin	Val McDermid
The Cleverness of Ladies	Alexander McCall Smith
Clouded Vision	Linwood Barclay
A Cool Head	Ian Rankin
A Cruel Fate	Lindsey Davis
The Dare	John Boyne
Dead Man Talking	Roddy Doyle
Doctor Who: Code of the Krillitanes	Justin Richards
Doctor Who: Magic of the Angels	Jacqueline Rayner
Doctor Who: Revenge of the Judoon	Terrance Dicks
Doctor Who: The Silurian Gift	Mike Tucker
Doctor Who: The Sontaran Games	Jacqueline Rayner
A Dreadful Murder	Minette Walters
A Dream Come True	Maureen Lee
The Escape	Lynda La Plante
Follow Me	Sheila O'Flanagan
Four Warned	Jeffrey Archer
Full House	Maeve Binchy
Get the Life You Really Want	James Caan
The Grey Man	Andy McNab
Hello Mum	Bernardine Evaristo

Hidden	Barbara Taylor Bradford
How to Change Your Life in 7 Steps	John Bird
Humble Pie	Gordon Ramsay
Jack and Jill	Lucy Cavendish
Kung Fu Trip	Benjamin Zephaniah
Last Night Another Soldier	Andy McNab
Life's New Hurdles	Colin Jackson
Life's Too Short	Val McDermid, Editor
The Little One	Lynda La Plante
Love is Blind	Kathy Lette
Men at Work	Mike Gayle
Money Magic	Alvin Hall
One Good Turn	Chris Ryan
Out of the Dark	Adèle Geras
Paris for One	Jojo Moyes
The Perfect Holiday	Cathy Kelly
The Perfect Murder	Peter James
Pictures Or It Didn't Happen	Sophie Hannah
Quantum of Tweed: The Man with the Nissan Micra	Conn Iggulden
Red for Revenge	Fanny Blake
Rules for Dating a Romantic Hero	Harriet Evans
A Sea Change	Veronica Henry
Star Sullivan	Maeve Binchy
Street Cat Bob	James Bowen
The 10 Keys to Success	John Bird
Tackling Life	Charlie Oatway
Today Everything Changes	Andy McNab
Traitors of the Tower	Alison Weir
Trouble on the Heath	Terry Jones
Twenty Tales from the War Zone	John Simpson
We Won the Lottery	Danny Buckland
Wrong Time, Wrong Place	Simon Kernick

Quick Reads

Start a new chapter

Out of the Dark

Adèle Geras

Rob Stone comes back from the horrors of the First World War with a ruined face and a broken heart. Lonely, unable to forget the things he has seen, and haunted by the ghost of his dead captain, all that Rob has left is a picture of the captain's family. Rob sets out to find them, hoping that by giving them the picture, he can bring peace to the captain's ghost – and to his own troubled heart.

Quercus

Quick Reads
Start a new chapter

Red for Revenge

Fanny Blake

Two women, one man: code red for revenge...

Maggie is married with two grown-up children. Her twenty-five year-old marriage to Phil has lost its sparkle.

Carla is widowed. She understands life is short so she lives it to the full. But is her new romance all that it seems?

When the two women meet in the beauty salon, they soon find they have more in common than the colour of their nails.

The discovery that they are sharing the same man is shocking. How will Phil be taught a lesson or two he won't forget?

Orion

Quick Reads

Why not start a reading group?

If you have enjoyed this book, why not share your next Quick Read with friends, colleagues, or neighbours.

A reading group is a great way to get the most out of a book and is easy to arrange. All you need is a group of people, a place to meet and a date and time that works for everyone.

Use the first meeting to decide which book to read first and how the group will operate. Conversation doesn't have to stick rigidly to the book. Here are some suggested themes for discussions:

- How important was the plot?
- What messages are in the book?
- Discuss the characters – were they believable and could you relate to them?
- How important was the setting to the story?
- Are the themes timeless?
- Personal reactions – what did you like or not like about the book?

There is a free toolkit with lots of ideas to help you run a Quick Reads reading group at **www.quickreads.org.uk**

Share your experiences of your group on Twitter @Quick_Reads

For more ideas, offers and groups to join visit Reading Groups for Everyone at **www.readingagency.org.uk/readinggroups**

Quick Reads

Other resources

Enjoy this book?

Find out about all the others at **www.quickreads.org.uk**

For Quick Reads audio clips as well as videos and ideas to help you enjoy reading visit the BBC's Skillswise website **www.bbc.co.uk/quickreads**

Skillswise

Join the Reading Agency's Six Book Challenge at **www.readingagency.org.uk/sixbookchallenge**

THE READING AGENCY

Find more books for new readers at
www.newisland.ie
www.barringtonstoke.co.uk

Barrington Stoke

Free courses to develop your skills are available in your local area. To find out more phone 0800 100 900.

National Careers Service
Helping you take the next step

For more information on developing your skills in Scotland visit **www.thebigplus.com**

the big plus

Want to read more? Join your local library. You can borrow books for free and take part in inspiring reading activities.

Quick Reads

Start a new chapter

The Booker Prize Foundation

Dead Man Talking is the result of Galaxy® Quick Reads and the Booker Prize Foundation working together.

The Booker Prize Foundation is a registered charity (no 1090049). Since 2002, it has awarded the Man Booker Prize for Fiction. This is one of the UK's oldest and most respected literary prizes.

Roddy Doyle won the Booker Prize in 1993 for his novel, *Paddy Clarke Ha Ha Ha*. He is the first Man Booker Prize author to write a Galaxy® Quick Read.

Roddy Doyle's Quick Read will expand the existing reach of the Foundation's Books Unlocked programme. This is part of the charity's commitment to building the bridge between literature and literacy.

With the help of the National Literacy Trust, Books Unlocked promotes literacy in prisons and young offender institutions. It is designed to engage prisoners in reading. The programme aims to increase their enjoyment of reading and to get prisoners reading more often. We hope, too, to introduce them to new books, nominated for the Man Booker Prize, which they might not have previously enjoyed.

www.themanbookerprize.com
www.literacytrust.org.uk/books_unlocked

The Booker Prize Foundation